Dear Evan,
I hope you enjoy reading this
book and find special people
and special frieds through out
long life voiage

Fond : Siddharth
August 14' 09

For Jacquie
C.F.

To all little children who love nature and animals such as bears,
the symbols of untouched and wild forests
D.K.

First published in Great Britain in 2007 by Gullane Children's Books
Text © Claire Freedman 2007
Illustrations © Dubravka Kolanovic 2007

This 2008 edition published by Sandy Creek
by arrangement with Gullane Children's Books

Sandy Creek, 122 Fifth Avenue, New York, NY 10011

ISBN-13: 978-1-4351-0921-6

10   8   6   4   2   1   3   5   7   9

Printed and bound in Indonesia

Little Bear's Special Friend

Claire Freedman • Dubravka Kolanovic

SANDY CREEK

One morning Little Bear woke from his deep, winter-long sleep.
"Hooray! It must be spring!" he cried excitedly.
Stretching and yawning, Little Bear peered out of his cave and blinked
in surprise. The woods were white with snow. Icicles hung from the trees.
"It's still winter!" gasped Little Bear. "I've woken up too soon!"
Little Bear burrowed down in his bed again, but he just couldn't sleep.

Little Bear's paws crunched deep
into the snow as he padded outside.
"Hello!" he shouted. "Is anyone awake?"
But the caves only echoed with deep rumbling
snores – his bear friends were still fast asleep.

Little Bear flopped down in the snow, feeling terribly lonely.
"I'll have no friends to play with until spring comes!" he said sadly.

"I'll be your friend!" called a voice.
Little Bear turned around in surprise. It was a little snowman!
"My name's Sparkly," laughed the snowman. "Cheer up, Little
Bear. Let me show you how much fun winter is!"

So Little Bear and Sparkly
skipped together through
the frosty woods,

and whizzed down
slippy-slidey snowdrifts.

They broke off icicles
to write their names
in the snow,

and caught tickly
snowflakes on the
tips of their tongues.
"Winter is fun, Sparkly!"
Little Bear said. "I'd like
to wake up early every year!"

One day, as they played, Little Bear
slid into a tree and was showered with snow.
"Look out!" he called. "I'm the Big Bad
Snowbear, and I'm coming to get you!"
And, giggling, Little Bear chased Sparkly
all through the snowy woods.

"You're my best friend forever!" Little Bear
whispered to Sparkly one dark night. Snowflakes
glittered like falling stars in the bright, white moonlight.
"You're MY best friend forever!" Sparkly smiled.
And they hugged each other tight.

At last the snow stopped falling. Sparkly showed Little Bear the other animals living in the woods.

"Little Bear!" called Tuft-tail squirrel. "Help me dig up the acorns I buried last autumn!"

"Little Bear! Sparkly!" shouted Flinty Fox. "Let's go skating on the ice!"

Little Bear had great fun
playing with Tuft-tail and Flinty.
But Sparkly was his special friend.

Little by little the days grew warmer . . .

Then, one day, Sparkly told Little Bear,
"Spring will be here soon, and I must go away!"
"GO AWAY?" cried Little Bear, shocked. "Why?"
"Because Little Bears sleep through winter, and in the spring Snowmen
go away to where the snow never melts," Sparkly said gently. "That's how it is."

"But that means we'll never
see each other again!" said Little Bear.
"Best friends always find a way of
being together!" Sparkly promised.
"You'll see, Little Bear!"

Then Sparkly and Little Bear held
each other close for a long, long time.

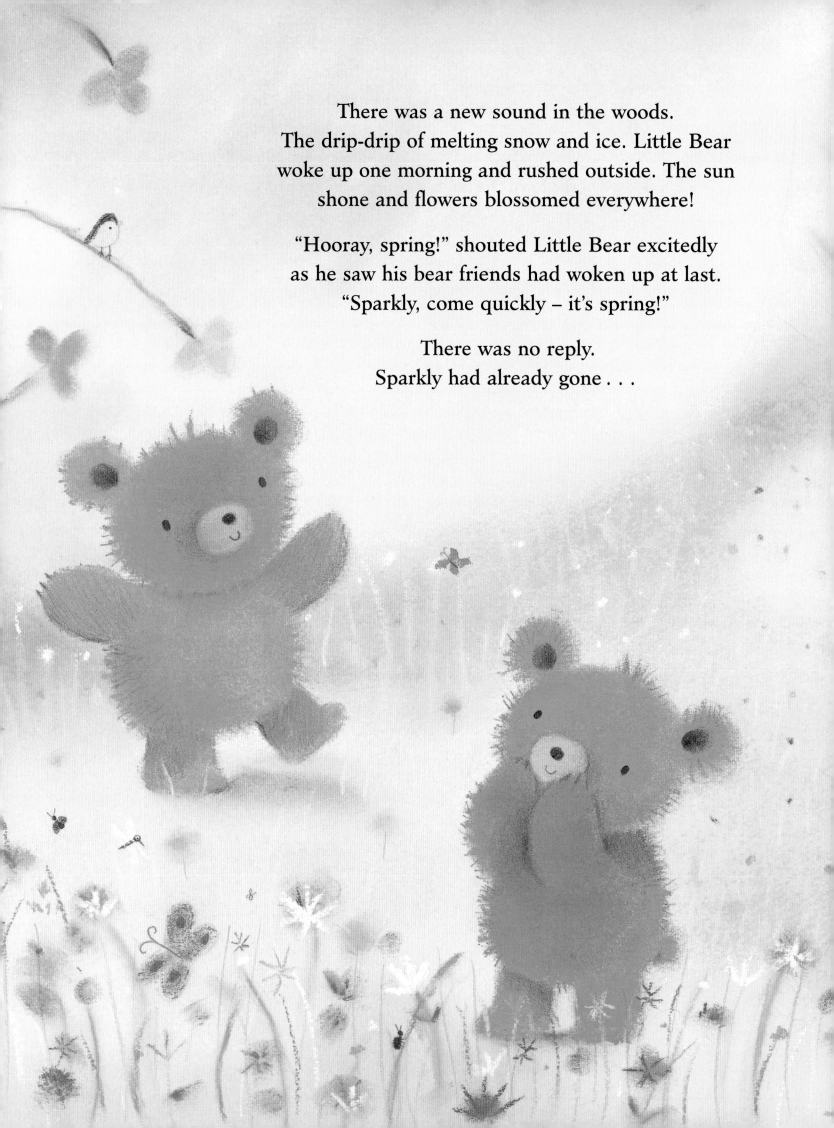

There was a new sound in the woods.
The drip-drip of melting snow and ice. Little Bear
woke up one morning and rushed outside. The sun
shone and flowers blossomed everywhere!

"Hooray, spring!" shouted Little Bear excitedly
as he saw his bear friends had woken up at last.
"Sparkly, come quickly – it's spring!"

There was no reply.
Sparkly had already gone . . .

"Goodbye, Sparkly," Little Bear whispered sadly. "I'll miss you."
"We all will," agreed Tuft-tail and Flinty.

Little Bear cheered up as he
played with his bear friends.
But as spring came and went,
he often thought about Sparkly.

When the bears climbed trees,
to get sticky, yummy, honey,
Little Bear laughed,
"Sparkly would love this!"

As they splashed
in the cool stream
on hot summer days,
he said, "Sparkly and
I ice-skated here."

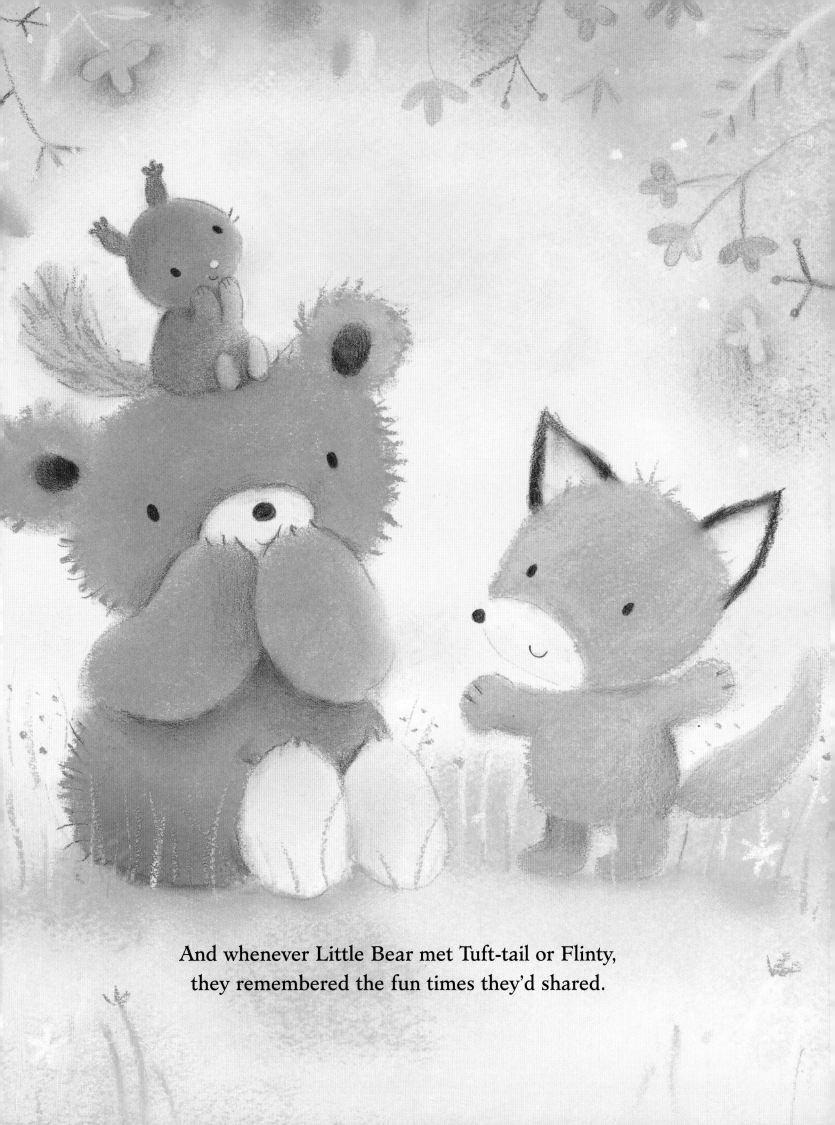

And whenever Little Bear met Tuft-tail or Flinty,
they remembered the fun times they'd shared.

Winter was on the way again. The bears filled their caves
with warm leaves, ready for their long winter sleep.
"See you next spring," they yawned.
"Sleep tight!" waved Little Bear.
"Don't let the bear-bugs bite!"

Soon he was fast asleep, too.
Little Bear slept . . . and slept . . .

. . . until he was stirred by someone's gentle nudging!
Little Bear opened his eyes.
"SPARKLY!"
"I woke you just a tiny bit early, Little Bear," Sparkly whispered.
"Best friends always find a way to be together!"
"They do!" cried Little Bear happily.

And, together, Little Bear and Sparkly skipped
outside,into the whirling, swirling, softly-falling snow.